You won't find me!

1, 2, 3, 4...

…5, 6, 7, 8, 9, 10!

ALFONSE, WHERE ARE YOU?

Linda Wikler

Crown Publishers, Inc., New York

For David and Alan

Published by Crown Publishers, Inc., a Random House company,
201 East 50th Street, New York, NY 10022

CROWN is a trademark of Crown Publishers, Inc.

Manufactured in Singapore

Library of Congress Cataloging-in-Publication Data
Wikler, Linda.
Alfonse, where are you? / by Linda Wikler. — 1st ed.
      p.   cm.
Summary: Alfonse the goose can't find Little Bird when they play
hide-and-seek, but if he were quiet, he might be able to hear her.
[1. Hide-and-seek—Fiction. 2. Geese—Fiction. 3. Birds—Fiction.]
I. Title.
PZ7.W6415Al   1996
[E]—dc20 95-3670

ISBN   0-517-70045-X (trade)
        0-517-70046-8 (lib. bdg.)

10 9 8 7 6 5 4 3 2 1

First Edition

Ready or not, here I come!

ALFONSE, WHERE

Alfonse was looking for a good hiding place, but...

no
tree
was
wide
enough,

no rock was big enough,

and no grass was tall enough.

So Alfonse kept looking.

Then he found a place,
and just in time.
Little Bird was coming!

The hiding place was <u>so</u> good, and Alfonse was <u>so</u> quiet, that Little Bird walked right past him!

Alfonse waited and waited.

Come out, come out, wherever you are!

But Little Bird didn't return.

HERE I AM!

honked Alfonse.

LITTLE BIRD,
WHERE ARE YOU?

**Hee,
hee,
hee!**

giggled Little Bird, but
Alfonse didn't hear her.

OH, NO! *said Alfonse.*
WHERE COULD LITTLE BIRD BE?

Alfonse began to look for Little Bird.

LITTLE BIRD!
LITTLE BIRD!

HELP! HELP! *he cried to the other geese.*
I've lost Little Bird!

The geese helped Alfonse look.

HONK!

HONK!

HONK!

HONK!

HONK!

Here I am!

said Little Bird.
But no one heard her.

Where are you, Little Bird?

So the geese looked in the water.

Here I am!
said Little Bird.
But <u>still</u> no one heard her.

Little Bird was tired of playing. She sat down by the lake to wait and soon fell asleep.

And that's just where Alfonse found her.

WOOPS!

LOOK, EVERYONE,
I FOUND LITTLE BIRD!

Shhh! *whispered Alfonse.*
She's sleeping!

I knew you would find me! *Little Bird said when she awoke.*

You were supposed
to find <u>me</u>!
said Alfonse.

Oh.

The next day, Little Bird asked to play hide-and-seek again.

Only if you promise
to find me this time!
said Alfonse.

I promise.

This time Alfonse found a very good hiding place.

I see you!

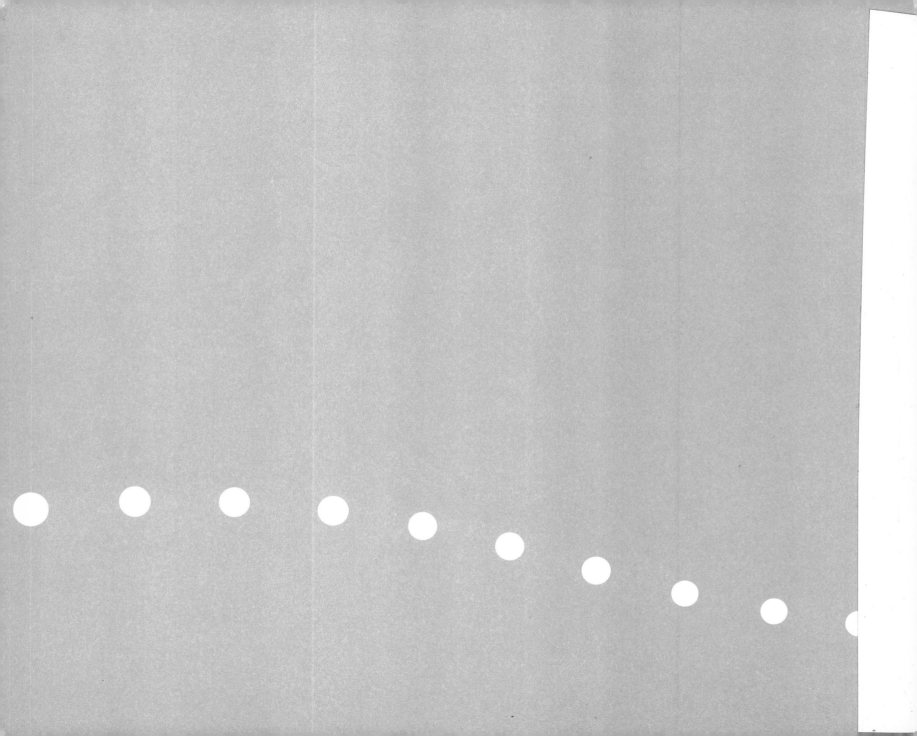